This book belongs to

_____

ISBN 978-1-4847-9029-8
FAC-038091-16204
Printed in the United States of America
Library of Congress Control Number: 2016936336
First Hardcover Edition, September 2016
10 9 8 7 6 5 4 3 2 1
For more Disney Press fun, visit www.disneybooks.com

SUSTAINABLE FORESTRY INITIATIVE Certified Sourcing
www.sfiprogram.org
SFI-00993
This Label Applies to Text Stock Only

DISNEY · PIXAR
FINDING DORY

Hide-and-Seek with Dory

By
Bonita Garr

Illustrated by the
Disney Storybook Art Team

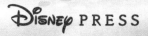

DISNEP PRESS
Los Angeles • New York

One . . . two . . . three . . .
um . . . four . . . um . . . um . . .

Hi, I'm Dory!
You're here just in time.

I was about to, uh . . .
Lie and sneak? No.
Spy and peek? No.

Do YOU know what I was about to do?

Hide-and-seek?

Oh, yeah! Boy, you're good.

Come on, let's go!
Point if you see anyone.

Did you just–
STOP!
DON'T TOUCH THAT!

Gee, that's funny.
Why would I say "Don't touch th—"

YEEOWCH!

Now I remember.

Anemones
STING!

What were we doing again

That's right! We're looking for—
Oh, hey . . .

Sand!

I like sand.
Sand is squishy.

Why are you looking
at me like that?
What did I forget?

Hide-and-seek?
I love that game!
I'll be it.
Do you see anyone hiding?

Hank?
I don't see him.
What color is he?

Yellow?
No.

Pink?
Nope, don't see him.

Brown?

Nope, not here, either.
Let's look over there.
Follow me!

Just keep swimming...
Just keep swimming...

Just keep—
hey . . .

Why are you
following me?

Oh! Ha! I told you to follow me because . . . look!

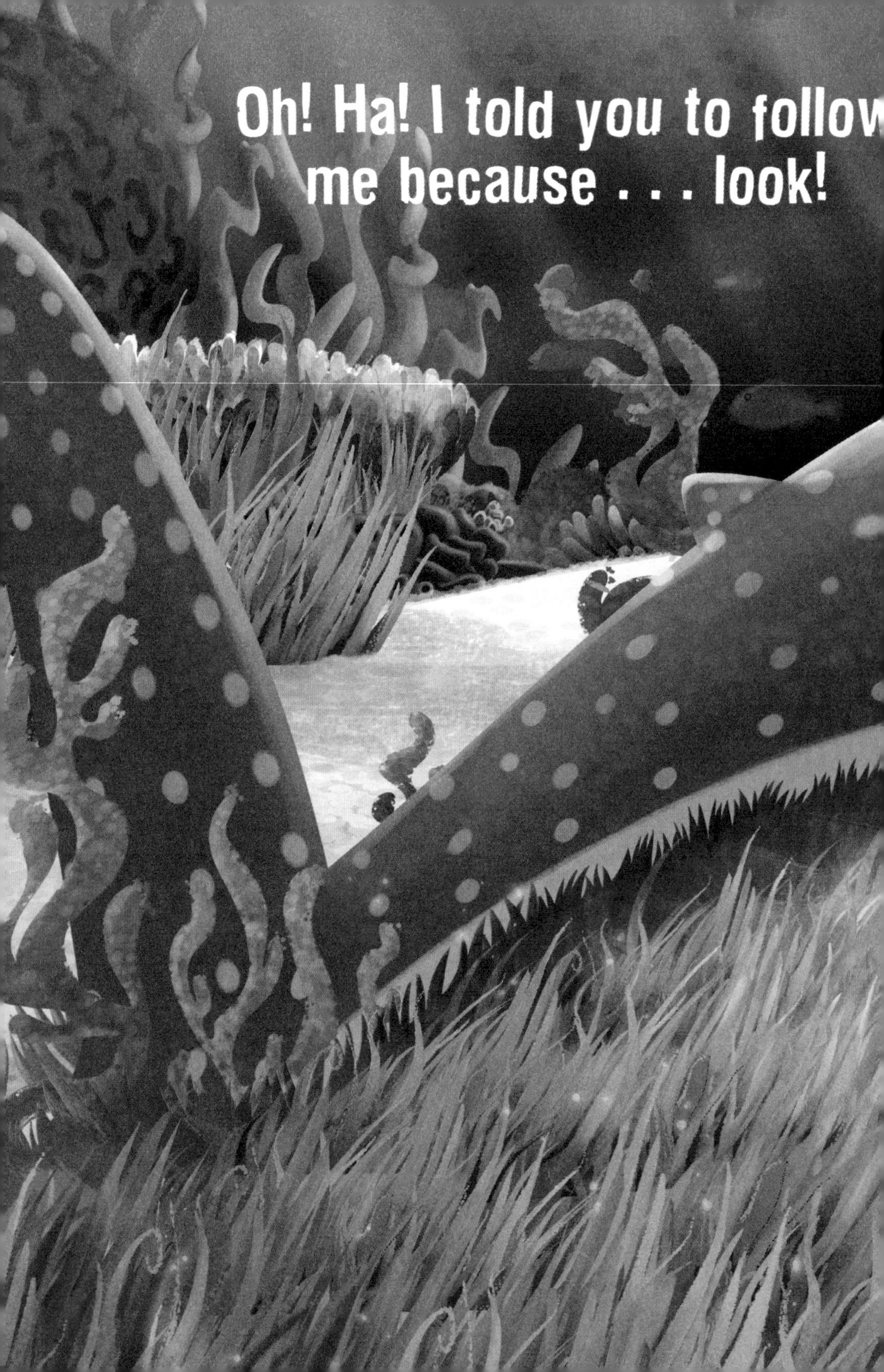

A pretty shell!

My mom loves shells!
But I haven't seen her
or my dad in a while.
Where are they?

WHAT?
We're playing hide-and-seek?
Nobody told me!

QUICK!

We'd better hide in here!

Mom! Dad! I found
this great hiding
spot. Come in, I'll
make room!

Hey, guys!
Get in here, before
someone finds you!

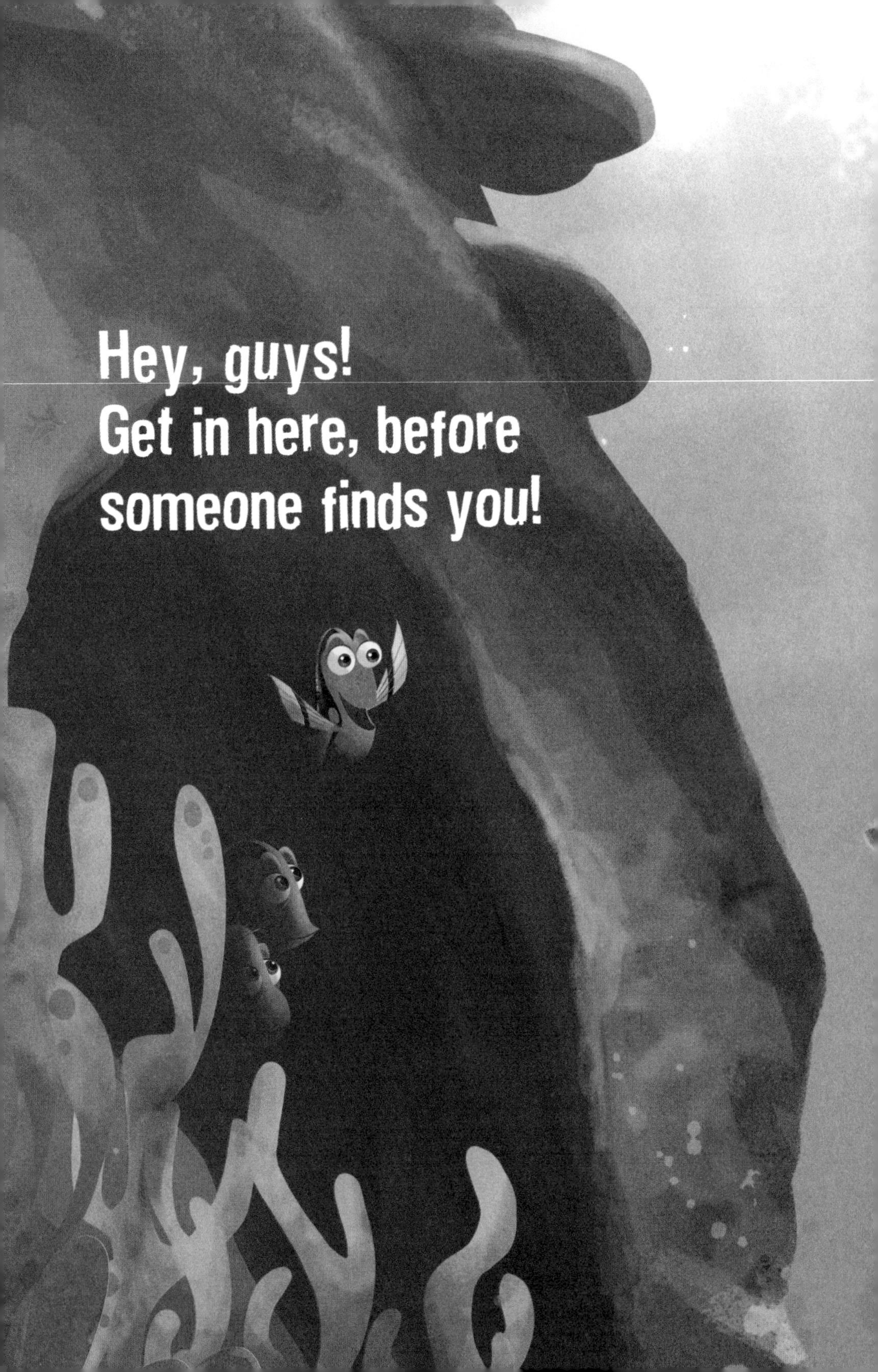

You guys, too?
It's gonna be tight.

Destiny, suck it in a bit.
Tail first, Bailey!

Okay, okay,
everybody in.
We can squeeze.

Nemo! Marlin!
We are . . .
What are we doing?

HIDE-AND-SEEK?

I'm it?
I'm looking for my friends?

I FOUND THEM!

Now what?
Let's play tag.
I'm it!

This is going to be great! Wait . . . what am I doing?

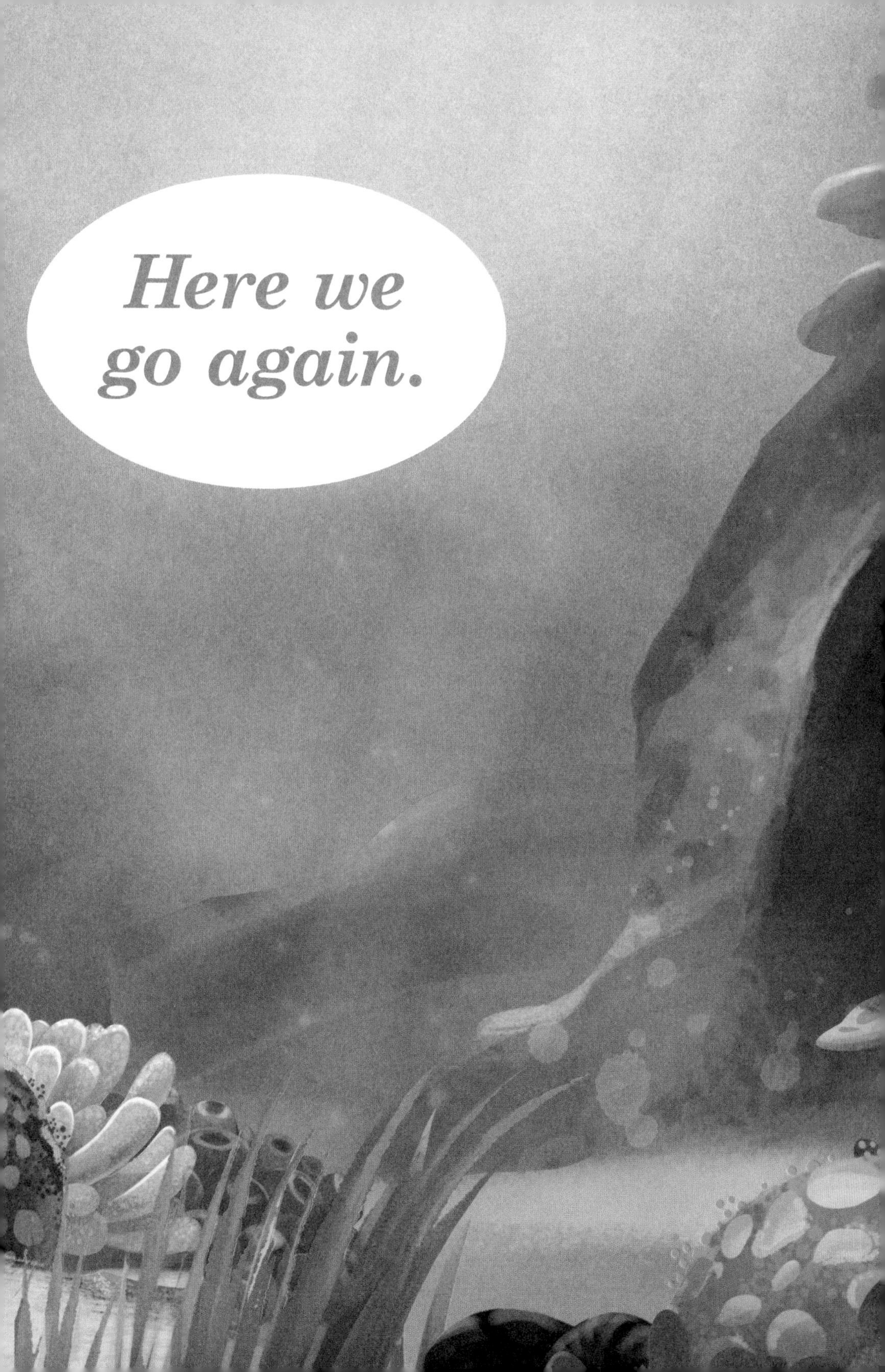
Here we go again.